DINOSAURS DANCE

By Larry Dane Brimner

Illustrated by Patrick Girouard

Children's Press®
A Division of Scholastic Inc.
New York • Toronto • London • Auckland • Sydney
Mexico City • New Delhi • Hong Kong
Danbury, Connecticut

For Jacob Keeser
–L. D. B.

For my friends at the White Oak School
–P. G.

Reading Consultant
Linda Cornwell
Learning Resource Consultant
Indiana Department of Education

Visit Children's Press® on the Internet at:
http://publishing.grolier.com

Library of Congress Cataloging-in-Publication Data
Brimner, Larry Dane.
Dinosaurs dance / by Larry Dane Brimner ; illustrated by Patrick Girouard.
p. cm. — (A rookie reader)
Summary: Though other animals may twirl and prance, there is nothing like a dinosaur dance.
ISBN 0-516-20752-0 (lib. bdg.)   0-516-26358-7 (pbk.)
[1. Dinosaurs—Fiction. 2. Dance—Fiction. 3. Stories in rhyme.] I. Girouard, Patrick, ill. II. Title. III Series.
PZ8.3.B77145Di 1998
[E] —dc21
97-18798
CIP
AC

All rights reserved. Published simultaneously in Canada
Printed in China
        8 9 10 R 07   62

Dinosaurs roar.

Dinosaurs rock.

Dinosaurs dip.

Dinosaurs . . . slip!

Dinosaurs sway.

Dinosaurs step.

Dinosaurs hop.

Dinosaurs . . . flop!

Dinosaurs twirl.

19

Dinosaurs twist.

Dinosaurs shuffle.

Dinosaurs . . . ruffle!

Dinosaurs clap.
Dinosaurs clog.

Dinosaurs prance.

Dinosaurs . . . DANCE!

Word List (17 words)

clap	hop	slip
clog	prance	step
dance	roar	sway
dinosaurs	rock	twirl
dip	ruffle	twist
flop	shuffle	

About the Author

Larry Dane Brimner lives in the southwest region of the United States. He writes on a wide range of topics, from picture book and middle-grade fiction to young adult nonfiction. His previous Rookie Readers include *Brave Mary, Firehouse Sal, How Many Ants?,* and *Lightning Liz.*

About the Illustrator

Patrick Girouard lives in Indiana. He has two beautiful sons called Marc and Max. He loves a red-haired lady, dogs, bagels, coffee, making pictures, naps, and many other things too numerous to mention.